More adventures of the

Pandora

PIRATE PRINCESS

PORTIA

JUDY BROWN

SIMON AND SCHUSTER

For Kate

SIMON AND SCHUSTER
First published in Great Britain by Simon & Schuster UK Ltd, 2006
A CBS COMPANY

1 3 5 7 9 10 8 6 4 2

Simon & Schuster UK Ltd
Africa House
64-78 Kingsway
London WC2B 6AH

A CIP catalogue record for this book is available from the British Library

ISBN 1 416 90190 6
EAN 9781416901907
Typeset by Ana Molina
Printed and bound in Great Britain by Cox & Wyman Ltd, Reading, Berkshire

Contents

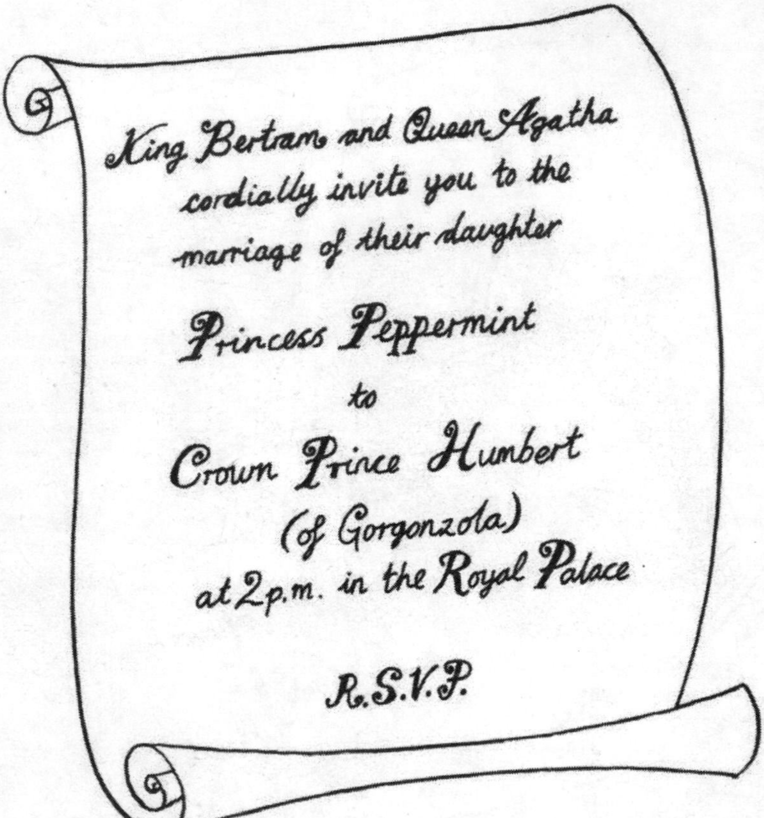

King Bertram and Queen Agatha
cordially invite you to the
marriage of their daughter

Princess Peppermint

to

Crown Prince Humbert
(of Gorgonzola)
at 2 p.m. in the Royal Palace

R.S.V.P.

Chapter One

Portia the Pirate Princess looked out of the window of the Captain's cabin on her pirate ship, the *Flying Pig*. As she watched, Squawk, her parrot, flew through the window and landed on the desk in front of her.

'Parrot post! Parrot post!' squawked Squawk.

'Thanks, Squawk,' said Portia, as she took the rolled-up piece of paper from Squawk's leg, but her face filled with dread as she read the note.

It was from Portia's cousin, Princess Peppermint. She and Portia were very close and they had been sending messages to each other ever since Portia had gone to sea.

'Jim!' she called out. 'Peppermint needs our help!'

Now, you may be wondering how a princess ends up captain of her own pirate ship. Once upon a time, Portia had been a normal, average type of princess, just like all the others. Well, not *exactly* like all the others. You may be surprised to hear that not *everybody* enjoys being a princess. After all, there's rather a lot of curtseying,

learning to sew, basket-weaving, flower- arranging, poetry reading, walking around with books balanced on your head and generally not speaking unless you're spoken to.

3

Portia, on the other hand liked rock-climbing, archery, woodwork, abseiling, scuba-diving and arguing with anyone who tried to make her do anything she didn't want to.

Then, one day, much to Portia's horror, her
father, King Bernard, presented her with a picture
of Prince Rupert. He was the
drippiest prince you could
ever have the misfortune to
meet - but he was the prince
that King Bernard had chosen
for Portia to marry. It was
the final straw.

Portia ran away the very next day with a
bunch of her ladies-in-waiting (who were tired of
just waiting around),

sold her crown,

bought a ship and set out to sea.

They sailed away in such a hurry that Jim, the
Flying Pig's cabin boy was still asleep in his bunk,
totally unaware that the ship had changed hands.

Luckily, Portia asked him to stay and help them learn how to sail the ship and, since his old captain had been a lot uglier, smellier and nastier than Portia, Jim had agreed.

That was all a while ago, but now Princess Peppermint was in the same sort of trouble.

'What is it, Captain P?' asked Jim, rushing into the cabin.

'Here, Jim, read this. We have to do something!'

Chapter Two

Dear Portia,

I have to write this quickly, before anybody comes. They've locked me in my room in case I try to run away like you did. Do you remember Prince Humbert? He was the laziest, stupidest and most miserable of all the princes at school and Daddy has decided that I must marry him! He can't even tie his own shoelaces without getting out of puff and he HATES exercise! What will I do if I can't keep up my training, I'll go CRAZY if I have to go and live in his palace. Please, please, help — there's not much time. I can hear someone coming and Squawk's waiting for the note. DON'T LET ME DOWN!

Love from your desperate cousin,

Princess Peppermint xx

'This is terrible!' shouted Portia. 'How long will it take to get to Tangerine Bay, Jim?'

Jim looked at the charts. 'Well, if we sail through the night and the winds stay strong, we should reach it just before dawn.'

Portia rushed outside. 'All hands on deck, all hands on deck!' she yelled. 'Ladies! We have a princess to rescue!'

While the *Flying Pig* sailed for Tangerine Bay, Portia made plans with the ladies-in-waiting.

Portia had chosen her ship carefully; it was small and fast, and just the right size to be run by a crew of girls. They all loved their life at sea. No one, except for Portia, of course, told them what to do any more. And it was fun!

'OK,' said Portia, 'this is a plan of the palace as far as I can remember it and here is Peppermint's bedroom. I'll need two of you to come with me and Jim, and we'll need plenty of rope.'

'I'd like to come, Captain,' said Able-seawoman

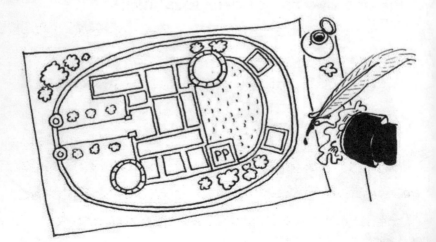

Anisha. 'I remember Prince Humbert visiting the palace once. He was revolting. The greedy pig ate

so many cream cakes that he was sick and I was the one who had to clear it up! Yuck.'

'I'll come too,' said Ship's Lookout, Emily, 'I like Princess Peppermint, she was always really friendly to us.' All of the other ladies-in-waiting agreed.

'Right, that's sorted then,' said Portia. 'You lot get the ropes and I'll sort out the rest of the stuff we'll need. Be ready to go ashore as soon as we reach Tangerine Bay. Squawk, take this note to

Peppermint so that she's ready for us and she knows the plan.'

'Aye, aye, Cap'n!' squawked Squawk.

The *Flying Pig* sailed through the night and arrived at Tangerine Bay, as Jim had predicted, just as the

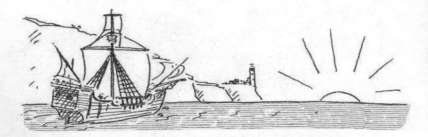

sun started to rise. They quickly dropped anchor away from the harbour, lowered the rowing boat and loaded it with equipment for the rescue.

'OK!' said Portia. 'Does everybody know what they're supposed to do?'

'Yes, Cap'n!' replied the crew confidently.

'Good. The rest of you stay aboard and keep your heads down, we don't want anybody getting suspicious. Right, Jim, let's go!' and with that they rowed away from the ship.

Chapter Three

Portia pulled her hat down to cover her face and looked around cautiously as they rowed to shore, Squawk sitting quietly on her shoulder. She stared at the ships in the harbour and a shiver ran down her spine.

'Jim,' she whispered, 'do any of those ships look familiar to you?'

Jim looked over at the ships moored in the harbour. 'No, I can't say they do, Captain P. Why do you ask?'

'I don't know really, it's just . . . oh well, I suppose one ship is pretty much like another, isn't it?'

Portia shrugged her shoulders and pulled a map out of her coat pocket. 'Look, this is where we have to go,' she said, pointing at the map.

'There's a big wall all around the outside of

the palace, so we're going to have some climbing
to do. We have to be careful that nobody spots us.
If the palace guards see me, they'll tell my uncle,
King Bertram, and the whole game will be up.'

The boat reached the shore with a bump and
Portia leapt out. She helped the others unload
their equipment, then tied up the boat and led
them away from the beach. They wove their way
through the undergrowth and into the woods
that led to the palace.

Before too long they had reached the palace walls. Portia pulled the map out once more. 'This way!' she said, and they crept around to the side where Peppermint's bedroom lay. 'OK, stop here. This is it.' All four of them crouched down behind some bushes.

'Right, Jim,' said Portia, 'could you give me the grappling hook?' Jim passed her the hook and Portia tied it to a length of rope. She swung it around her head and up towards the castellations on top of the palace wall.

'Great shot!' whispered Jim, as the hook grabbed onto the wall.

'Thanks, Jim.' Portia smiled proudly. 'OK. Anisha and Emily, you two stay here and keep watch while Jim and I climb up the rope. If anyone comes, give two short blows on this whistle to warn us.'

Portia and Jim shinned up the rope, trying not to look down. Finally they reached the top. They climbed over the wall and pulled the rope up behind them. Squawk flew up to join them, landing on Portia's shoulder.

'That's Peppermint's window over there,' said Portia, pointing to a window almost opposite,

'Here, Squawk, fly over and give her this note.'

NEVER FEAR,
PORTIA'S HERE!
STAND AWAY FROM
THE WINDOW!

Squawk did as Portia asked and she and Jim
watched as the parrot disappeared through the
window. Suddenly they
saw Peppermint's excited
face appear at the
opening and she gave a
thumbs-up sign, before
stepping away from the
window.

'Here goes!' cried Portia, as she raised her bow and arrow and aimed at the window.

TWANG! went the bow and the arrow flew straight as a die through Peppermint's bedroom window, followed by the piece of string attached to it. Jim and Portia heard a small cheer and Peppermint appeared at the window holding the string triumphantly.

'OK, Jim, let's tie the string to this rope so that Peppermint can pull it across,' said Portia.

Jim followed her instructions and, on Portia's signal, Peppermint started to pull.

'I've told Princess Peppermint to tie that end securely somewhere in her room and we must do the same this end. It's got to be as tight as we can make it, because Peppermint's going to walk across it,' explained Portia.

'*What?*' exclaimed Jim. 'That's impossible, it's much too far − she'll fall!'

'Oh no, she won't,' said Portia, smiling. 'You don't know Princess Peppermint: she could do it with her eyes closed. Don't worry, just watch.'

Just as Portia finished speaking, out of the window
climbed Princess Peppermint, still wearing her
pyjamas. The King hadn't put any guards on her
window since it was six floors up. Peppermint
stepped elegantly onto the rope, her arms out-
stretched on either side for balance.

Following close behind her was a scrawny-looking Siamese cat, not looking quite as confident as the Princess. Slowly but steadily, Peppermint placed one foot in front of the other, while the Siamese wobbled along unsurely behind her.

'Come on, Twiggy, you can do it. Just don't look

down,' Princess Peppermint whispered. But Twiggy wasn't listening and, with a pitiful squeak, she leapt forward and grabbed onto Peppermint's leg.

'*Whooaa!!!*' It was Peppermint's turn to wobble.

'I can't watch!' whimpered Jim, hiding his face in his hands.

'Don't worry, she'll be fine,' Portia said, trying to reassure herself as much as Jim. 'There, look.'

Princess Peppermint had regained her balance and was now walking smoothly the rest of the way, with her cat sitting on her head like a turban.

'Portia, how can I ever thank you enough!' Peppermint gushed, as she leapt into Portia's arms. Portia hugged her cousin tightly and looked down at the trembling cat.

'So, who's this?' she asked.

'Oh! I hope you don't mind. I have to bring Twiggy with me, Daddy's allergic to cats so I can't leave her here.'

'I don't think it's me you have to worry about . . .' Portia said, nodding at Squawk, who was perched on her shoulder, looking very put out. 'Her name certainly suits her though!' she added, looking down at the skinny little cat. Twiggy was now rubbing herself against Portia's leg and looking pleadingly up at her. 'OK, OK, we'll get you some food – but first let's get out of here! It won't be long before they discover the two of you are missing.'

Portia lassoed a tree opposite the castle wall and the three of them swung down, with Peppermint's cat clinging on to her for all she was worth. They met up with Emily and Anisha and started back to the ship.

'By the way, Portia,' puffed Peppermint as they ran through the trees, 'do you remember Count Nasty?'

'How could I forget him! Nasty by name and nasty by nature. He worked for Prince Rupert's father.' Portia frowned at the memory.

'He's still searching for you, you know. Has been ever since you ran away. You'd better be careful - he's a really nasty piece of work.'

Portia began to feel uneasy.

Just then they heard an alarm sound in the distance and lots of shouting.

'Looks like they've found out you're missing,' she yelled. 'We'd better get a move on!'

A few minutes later they emerged onto the beach and, to their relief, the rowing-boat was bobbing just where they'd left it. Jim and Portia pushed the boat into the water, they all scrambled aboard and rowed as fast as their arms would let them back to the ship.

'It looks very quiet,' said Jim uneasily, looking over his shoulder at the *Flying Pig*, 'I can't see anyone at all.'

'Well, I did tell them to keep their heads down. I suppose they're just following orders,' said Portia.

They reached the ship and climbed back on-board but there was still no one to be seen.

'Where has everybody gone?' exclaimed Portia.

'Well, good morning, Princess Portia!' said a tall, dark figure, suddenly emerging from the shadows, 'So nice to see you after all this time.'

'COUNT NASTY! What the . . .'

'Grab them, men!'

And six burly sailors ran out from their hiding places to grab Portia and her friends.

Chapter Four

'So it was *your* ship I saw in the harbour! I knew
it seemed familiar,' Portia groaned, as a sailor
held her arms behind her back.

'Yes! How silly of me to leave it where you might see it,' said Count Nasty. 'But how fortunate for me that you didn't realise before! I knew you would come to rescue your cousin. Such a pity you've failed.' He smiled smugly. 'Now my crew will sail your ship back to meet Prince Rupert and you and Princess Peppermint can have a double wedding celebration!'

Portia's jaw dropped in horror.

'Won't that be lovely?' said Count Nasty, bending down to sneer at Portia. He was so close, his pointed beard was tickling her nose.

'*Achoooo!*' sneezed Portia, right in his face. The others sniggered.

Count Nasty wheeled around, wiping his face with his sleeve. 'And you won't find it quite so funny when King Bernard gets hold of you, either!' he snarled, waving his arm threateningly at Portia's companions. 'Take them below and lock them up!'

Count Nasty's men dragged Portia and the others down to the storeroom.

'Join the rest of your pathetic girly crew!' said one particularly unpleasant-looking sailor. He pushed them into the storeroom and locked the door.

Now the ladies-in-waiting really began to panic. Count Nasty had told them his plans and none of them wanted to go back to dry land – or to waiting. They loved their life of freedom on the ocean waves.

'What are we going to do, Captain?'

'I'll just die if we have to go back!'

'My Mum will be so mad with me, I'll be grounded for life!'

'It's a disaster!'

Some of the ladies-in-waiting even burst into tears.

'QUIET!' roared Portia. 'All of you just calm down - I'll think of something. We must use our brains. We can't overpower them, even with Jim on our side: they're just too strong. We'll have to outwit them and, judging by the look of them, that shouldn't be too difficult. Now, let's see what we've got in the storeroom. . . .'

They searched the room high and low for anything that might be useful and Jim and Peppermint made a list.

'So, what have we got?' asked Portia.

'Not much I'm afraid, Portia,' said Peppermint. 'There are some old nets, ropes and sails. Some elastic, barrels of fish, tins of flour, bits and pieces of wood and some black boot polish! I don't think any of that is going to help very much.'

'We're doomed, I tell you. DOOMED!' wailed Lady Donatella.

'Oh, do be quiet, I'm trying to think,' said Portia, though if she was truly honest her mind was a blank, but she knew she had to keep their spirits up.

Portia sat down on a pile of ropes and wracked her brains.

As she looked up at the hopeful, expectant faces around her, she noticed a chink of light coming from the corner of the storeroom, behind the barrels of fish. She ran over to the barrels.

'Jim, help me move these!' Portia cried.

They moved the barrels away from the corner to reveal a small hole in the wall.

Suddenly, Portia had a brainwave.

'OK, everyone. I think I've got a plan.'

Chapter Five

'Look!' said Portia. 'If we can get the spare keys from Jim's cabin, we can get in and out of the storeroom without Count Nasty or his crew knowing, and if we can do that then we can pick them off one by one.'

'Yes, but how does one of us get out of here to get the keys in the first place?' asked Jim, puzzled.

'Through this hole, of course.'

'But it's tiny, Captain. It's much too small for any of us to get through.'

'Not for Peppermint, it isn't,' said Portia, smiling.

Everyone looked at Princess Peppermint.

Princess Peppermint looked at the hole. 'You're right, you know! I'm sure I can get through there,' she said at last. 'Just tell me what to do when I get out!'

'Excellent,' said Portia. 'Squawk, fly out through here and find out how many men Count Nasty has brought with him. Peppermint and I have some planning to do!'

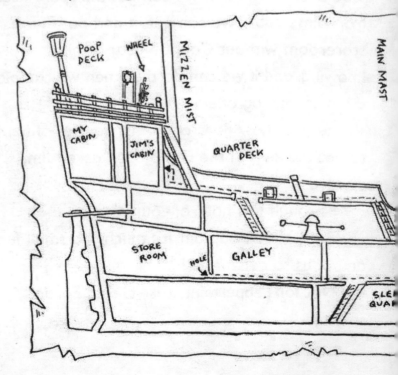

Portia drew a cross-section of the *Flying Pig*.

'OK, Peppermint, here's what you have to do. Once you get through into the galley next door, you'll have to get up on deck. Jim's cabin is at the other end of the ship, so how you get there will be down to you. The spare keys are on a hook beside his cabin door. Bring them straight back here as soon as you've got them.'

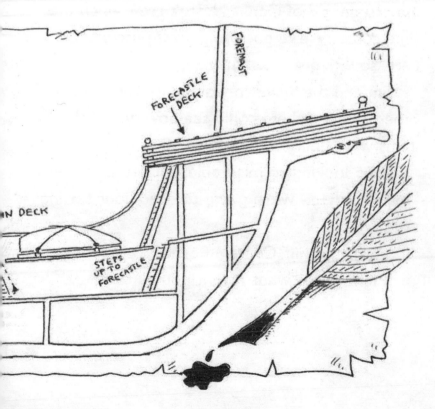

'No problem,' said Peppermint. 'I'll take this with me,' she added, rolling up the map.

'Let's wait until it gets dark,' said Portia, 'it'll be safer. We can't afford for you to get caught, or we're all done for!'

Just then, Squawk returned in a flurry of feathers, his mission accomplished.

'Right, now all we have to do is figure out how to get rid of Count Nasty's crew when the time comes. We've got some pretty useful stuff here, so let's get our thinking caps on.'

Jim and the ladies-in-waiting looked at each other. None of them could see how any of the items were going to be of use.

'Stop looking so miserable, you lot. Donatella, stop snivelling - we're going to need your sewing skills.'

'Aye, aye, *sniff*, Captain Portia.'

'Right, this is what I want you all to do . . .'

Chapter Six

As the sun went down, Peppermint prepared for her mission. She'd tied the rolled-up map to some string and slung it over her shoulder, just in case she forgot where to go.

'Good luck,' said Portia. 'I know you can do it, just be careful.'

'I will,' said Peppermint, looking a little nervous. 'See you soon, everyone!'

Portia and Jim pulled the barrels away from the wall to give Peppermint more room to get through. It was a tight squeeze but, with a bit of puffing and panting, she finally popped out the other side. She stuck her head back through the hole and waved goodbye. They all wanted to cheer, but managed to stay quiet. Just as she

disappeared from view, Twiggy suddenly dashed
for the hole, realising that she'd been left behind.

'Quick!' said Portia urgently. 'Stop the cat!
She'll give Peppermint away.'

But it was too late. Twiggy was too fast and
too skinny to catch. She darted between them all,

squeezed past the barrels and jumped through
the hole in the wall in pursuit of her Princess.

'Oh no!' groaned Portia. 'She's bound to lead
them straight to Peppermint.'

Donatella started to cry again.

'Maybe she'll just keep out of the way,' said Jim, hopefully. 'She's not exactly brave is she?'

'Let's hope she does,' replied Portia, sighing.

In the ship's galley, Princess Peppermint stood up and brushed the dust off her pyjamas. As she looked down she saw a familiar shape.

'Oh, Twiggy!' she whispered. 'You weren't supposed to follow me!'

Twiggy looked hurt.

'Never mind. It's nice not to be on my own - just stay close and don't make any noise.'

Twiggy purred quietly.

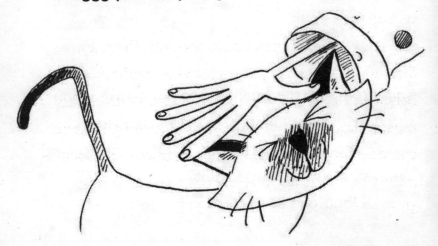

Peppermint squashed herself flat against the wall and looked around the room. In the far corner she could see a shadowy figure fast asleep in a chair.

That must be the cook, thought Peppermint. She dropped silently to her knees and crawled behind the table in the middle of the room, followed closely by Twiggy. Then she did forward rolls to the door, looked through the keyhole to make sure there was no one about, opened it and slipped outside.

'Now, according to the map,' she said to herself, 'I have to go up those stairs to get on deck.'
She glanced up to see two of Count Nasty's
sailors playing cards on a barrel just inches from
the top of the stairs.

'Bother!' Peppermint groaned. 'I'll have to find
another way.' She looked around. Behind her
were some more stairs. Very quietly she took out

the map. 'Those stairs will take me to the forecastle
deck, but that's even *further* away from where I
need to go.' She looked up at the sails.

Maybe ... she thought.

Silently, Peppermint crept up the steps behind

her and poked her head gingerly out of the hatch.

'No one there, good!' she whispered to herself. She looked up at the sails. 'It's the only way to go,' she said to Twiggy, 'you just stay here and keep watch.'

With a deep breath, Peppermint began to climb the sail's rigging and before too long she'd reached the top.

'That was the easy bit,' she said to herself. She still had to get across the rigging to the main-sail in the centre of the ship.

'Here goes!' Peppermint hooked her legs around the rope attached to the main sail and grabbed on tightly with her hands.

Slowly but surely she edged her way across. She could see the tops of the sailor's heads many metres below her, but decided it was better not to look down.

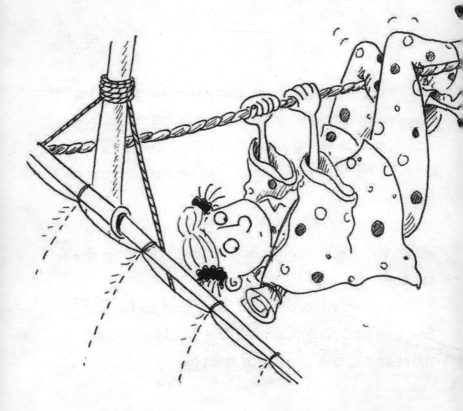

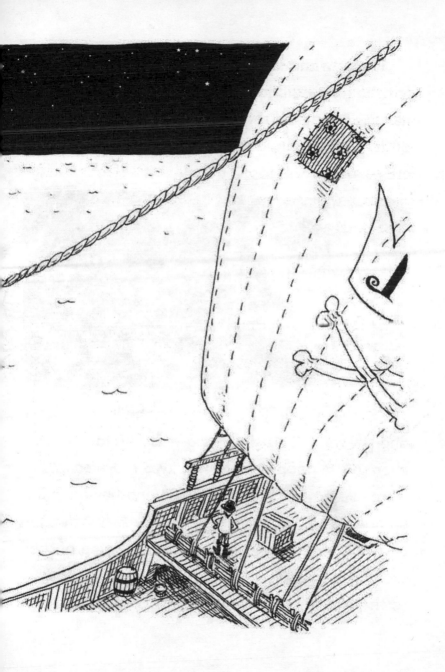

It was with huge relief that Peppermint finally felt the main-sail flapping around her feet, telling her she'd reached the mizzen mast. She grabbed on to it thankfully and pulled herself up into the crow's nest.

'Phew!' sighed Peppermint as she looked down and saw how high she really was. She looked over to the poop deck, where two more sailors were talking and drinking, while another patrolled up and down. Peppermint had to time her descent carefully. She swung her legs over the side of the crow's nest and grabbed a rope which led down to the quarterdeck. 'One, two, three, *go!*'

Peppermint slid down the rope, trying not to singe her pyjamas, and landed with a thump in the corner of the deck, knocking over a bucket of dirty water.

'What was that? Was that you, Bill?' called one of the sailors on the poop deck.

'Wasn't me, Crusher,' said Bill, the sailor who was on patrol. 'I thought it was you . . .'

Peppermint froze.

'Better take a look. I suppose,' said the man called Crusher, standing up and stretching.

Peppermint sped across the deck on tiptoe

towards Jim's cabin. She could hear Count Nasty
giving orders in Portia's cabin next-door and, with
her heart pounding in her chest, she opened Jim's
door just a crack, to check there was no one
there, and slipped inside. Peppermint rested her
back against the door, heart pumping as she got
her breath back, then looked around the room.

There, hanging on a hook by the door, just as
Portia had said, were the spare keys to all of the
doors and locks on the ship. Peppermint wrapped
them carefully in a pillowcase so that they wouldn't
rattle, then tied them around her waist.

Suddenly, Peppermint heard a knock on the door of Portia's cabin.

'Come in,' growled Count Nasty.

Peppermint looked through a crack in the door, as Bill and Crusher went inside.

'We heard strange noises!' said Bill as he went in.

'And someone knocked a bucket over,' added Crusher.

'Now's my chance,' said Peppermint to herself.

She crept out of Jim's cabin and back onto the quarterdeck, where Twiggy had come to meet her.

The cat rubbed her face against Peppermint's legs, delighted to see her mistress was safe. The two sailors were still playing cards near the steps.

'If only I could distract them somehow…' muttered Peppermint. Hearing this, Twiggy leapt

into action. She began to howl like only cats can and jumped up and ran straight across the barrel, knocking the sailors' cards all over the deck.

'Stupid cat! Where did that come from?' said one of the sailors, falling backwards off his seat.

'Something must have spooked it!' said the other, crawling over the deck picking up the cards.

In the commotion, Peppermint back-flipped her way past, leapt down the stairs and found herself back at the door of the galley, with Twiggy once again by her side.

'Nearly there!' she said to Twiggy and listened at the door. She could still hear the cook snoring like a pig, so she opened the door of the galley and went inside.

Chapter Seven

Meanwhile, back in the storeroom, Portia had put everyone to work.

'Two of you sort out these old sails: we need a pretty big one so if it needs mending, that's a job for Donnatella. Emily, collect all those pieces of wood together and find some strong string. Jim, bring that elastic over here and I'll show you what I want you to do.'

Portia showed Jim how make a catapult out of the wood, string and elastic.

'These are brilliant!' said Jim, twanging the elastic. 'But what are we going to use for ammunition?'

Portia grinned. 'Wait and see!' she said.

Just then there was a scratching sound from the corner of the storeroom.

'Captain, Captain, they're back!' called Anisha.

Peppermint emerged from the gloom smiling triumphantly, with Twiggy just behind.

'Here, we've got the keys,' said Peppermint, 'and we nicked some bread and cheese from the galley on the way back!'

'You're a star!' exclaimed Portia, giving her cousin a big hug. 'We were worried that Twiggy was going to give you away.'

'Actually, she was great! I don't know if I'd have got back without her help,' said Peppermint, stroking her cat affectionately.

They were almost as pleased with the bread and cheese as they were with the keys, as they hadn't eaten for ages.

'As soon as we've had something to eat we need to set things in motion,' said Portia. 'According to Squawk there are eight crew altogether, including the cook. I've worked out a plan to get rid of most of them, we just need to be organised.'

Out on deck the sailors were feeling uncomfortable.

'Something scared that cat I tell you; it just ran across the cards for no reason at all!' said Bones, one of the card players.

'Me and Bill heard noises up on the quarterdeck,' said Crusher. 'We told Count Nasty but he said we were just being stupid.'

The ship's cook, having woken from his after-dinner nap, came blundering up the stairs, shouting and with a face like thunder.

'Who's eaten all the bread and cheese? That was for breakfast, you greedy lot. I'm not baking any more now, so you'll just have to have porridge in the morning. And there's no jam to have in it neither!'

The crew looked blankly at each other.

'None of us have even been in the galley, Cookie,' said Crusher, 'not since dinner anyway.'

'Well, *somebody's* taken the grub,' snarled Cookie.

'Someone or . . . something,' said Bones.

They all shivered.

'If you ask me,' whispered Bones, 'this ship's haunted.'

'Maybe it's them stupid girls. Maybe they got out somehow,' suggested Crusher.

'Oh yeah! And got back in and locked themselves up again,' jeered Bones.

'That's it! I'm going to talk to the Count,' said Cookie. 'He'll get to the bottom of this.'

In the storeroom, Portia and the others heard a commotion.

'Quick, hide everything!' said Portia. 'Turn the lamps down. Pretend to be asleep. Someone's coming!'

They heard Count Nasty's voice up on deck and the footsteps of several of the crew.

'Look, you fools,' the Count was saying. 'They'll be exactly where you left them, there's no way they could have got out.' The footsteps grew closer and Count Nasty held a lamp up at the window in the door. 'SEE? There they are. Safely

locked-up and dreaming of their princes, no doubt. Heh, heh, heh!'

'It's ghosts, I tell you!' said Bones. 'I said it all along!'

The sailors rumbled their agreement.

'QUIET!!' roared Count Nasty. 'I'm beginning

to wonder which crew is the bigger bunch of girls! Now, stop all this nonsense and carry on with your duties. I'm going to bed!' And with that, he stormed off.

Count Nasty's crew skulked off. Some went to their sleeping quarters, while those on duty went back to their posts, but they were no happier and just as scared.

The storeroom, on the other hand, was full of stifled giggles. Portia was laughing so much that tears were streaming down her face.

'Poor things!' she squeaked. 'They'll have nightmares!' But they'd given her an idea of how to complete her plan.

'Attention, everybody!' said Portia, wiping away the tears. 'It's time for stage one of Operation Mutiny!'

Chapter Eight

Portia, Jim and Peppermint filled their pockets and some small sacks with as many herrings as they could cram in. They slung the sacks over their shoulders and stepped carefully out of the storeroom, followed by two of the ladies-in-waiting carrying an old sail.

They crept along the deck, staying in the shadows, until they got to where Crusher and Bill were keeping watch.

At the other end of the ship, Squawk dive-bombed Bones, Boots and another shipmate to create a diversion.

On Portia's signal, the whole of her crew got out their catapults and took aim.

'FIRE!' ordered Portia, and started firing herrings at the poor, confused sailors.

'*Aaaaargh*! Help! It's raining fish! *Owp!*' said Bill, as Portia catapulted a herring straight into his mouth.

'I can't seeee!' said Crusher, blinded by the sudden attack of flying fish.

The two sailors stumbled across the deck, followed by Portia, Jim and Petticoat, still firing the slippery, smelly fish for all they were worth. The ladies-in-waiting ran behind the sailors with the sail, ready to pounce.

'What's going on?' shouted Bill.

'I don't know, let's get out of here!' answered Crusher, slipping on a pile of fish and landing on his face. 'Help, me Bill!' he yelled.

'I'm coming, Crusher. Don't panic!'

Bill felt his way over to his shipmate and

helped him to his feet. Portia and the others advanced towards them, still catapulting their fishy ammunition, forcing Bill and Crusher to where the ladies-in-waiting were lying in wait.

'Now!' shouted Portia, and the ladies threw the sail over the top of Bill and Crusher, rolled them over and over, wrapping them up like a sausage roll.

'It must be a bit smelly in there with all those fish!' sniggered Jim.

'Serves them right,' said Portia, smiling.

'They shouldn't mess with me!'

They dragged the sailor sausage roll below decks and bundled it into the storeroom.

'Quick!' said Portia to the others in the storeroom, 'Get these two tied up and keep them quiet. Jim, bring that empty barrel and come with us.'

Jim rolled the empty fish barrel out of the storeroom and they both carried it up on deck.

'Right, Jim! You remember the next part of the plan?'

'Yes, Captain! Just make sure you aim properly. If you miss I'm going to be in big trouble.' He looked a little nervous.

'No problem,' said Peppermint. 'It'll be a doddle.'
Portia and Peppermint climbed the rigging, carrying the barrel between them. When they reached half way, they stopped and waited.

'We're ready, Jim!' whispered Portia and gave Jim a signal.

Jim sneaked over to the ship's bell, grabbed the string and rang it furiously.

Bones, who was on the poop deck with another shipmate, heard it.

'Who's ringing the bell down there?' he shouted. 'Stop messing about, Bill! BILL, CRUSHER, why
are you ringing the bell?'

There was no answer.

'Go on, Boots. See what they're up to,' Bones
said to his shipmate.

'Why should I go?'

The bell rang again.

'Because I say so and I'm in charge,' said Bones.

'You're just a scaredy cat,' said Boots,
'I suppose you think it's those ghosts again!'
he laughed.

'Of course I don't, it's just . . . well . . . I should
stay here in case . . . erm . . . in case Count Nasty
needs protecting.'

'HAH!' jeered Boots. 'OK, OK, I'll go. They're
probably just messing about, or it's the wind or
something. Won't be long.'

Boots marched his way down the stairs to the
main deck. He walked along the deck until he felt
something under foot.

'What on earth ...?' Boots looked down and saw that the whole of the deck was covered with fish. They were all over the place. On the deck, in the rigging, in the rowing-boat, everywhere. Boots looked around, scratching his head, as Portia and Peppermint watched him from directly above.

'Is anybody there?' he called. 'Bill? Crusher? Where did all these fish come from? Where are you?' Boots was completely baffled. He turned to call Bones.

'Oi, Bones, there's something funny going on. The ship's all covered with . . .' but before he could get to the end of his sentence, Portia and Peppermint dropped the barrel.

'Bullseye!' said Portia. It had landed right on top of Boots and trapped him inside.

'Help! Help!' yelled the muffled voice from inside the barrel. 'It's all gone dark!' He waddled round the deck, bumping into things like some demented wooden penguin, until Jim jumped out, knocked the barrel over and rolled it along the deck with a loud rumble. It sounded like thunder. Portia and Peppermint clambered down the rigging and ran down the stairs after Jim as he *bump, bump, bumped* the barrel down the steps.

Just as they reached the bottom they heard Bones' voice. He'd finally plucked up enough courage to come looking for his shipmates.

'Bill, Crusher, Boots? Where are you all? Was that thunder?'

But of course there was no reply.

'Oooer!' said Bones, as he looked around at the fish scattered everywhere. 'This is getting really weird!' He turned around and ran back down to the other end of the ship.

Chapter Nine

Portia, Petticoat and Jim rolled the once empty
barrel back into the storeroom.

'Put him with the others,' said Portia.

The ladies-in-waiting lifted the barrel off the
very dazed looking sailor, tied him up and settled
him down with the rest of his shipmates. The
three of them sat in the corner bound and
gagged, wondering what was going to happen
next.

'Well done, everybody. That's three down -
only five to go. We'll give them a little time to
calm down then we'll start part three of the plan.
Donna, get the sewing kit ready.'

Donnatella looked terrified.

They waited until all seemed quiet, then unlocked the door again.

'Stay in the shadows, Donnatella, and follow me. Jim will be right behind you. We're going down to the sleeping quarters.'

They crept towards the stairs and looked down into the room full of hammocks.

'Can you hear anything, Jim?' asked Portia.

'Only snoring. Sound's like there's a whole sty full of pigs down there.' Jim sniggered.

'Down we go then, but quietly.'

They tiptoed down the stairs and looked at the hammocks gently swinging with the movement of the ship. Incredibly, considering the noise of the snoring, only two of the hammocks were occupied. Portia went into the room.

'Over here, Donnatella.'

Donna slipped past one of the sleeping sailors to join Portia, who was standing next to a hammock occupied by his snoring shipmate.

'Jim,' said Portia, 'you keep guard while we work!'

Portia helped as Donnatella began to sew the edges of the hammock together. In and out, from one side to the other, until the sailor was tightly sewn up inside.

'It's a good job he's a heavy sleeper!' whispered Portia.

Donnatella almost smiled.

'OK. Now for the other one.'

They moved across to the other sleeping sailor and set to work again. They'd just begun to

sew the hammock together when the sailor sat
bolt upright.

'WHAT! WHO! WHERE! What's going on . . .'

Portia and Donnatella dropped to the floor
under the hammock, praying that he wouldn't
look down. Jim jumped back into the shadows
and held his breath.

The sailor looked around him in the gloom.
He could just make out the shape of his shipmate
in the other hammock, but not that he'd become
part of the hammock itself.

'Must've been dreaming. Hmmmm . . .' he said sleepily, sucking his thumb and settling back down into his hammock.

Portia looked at Donna, who was shaking like a leaf and as white as a sheet. She held her hand to reassure her and, when the sailor started to snore again, the two of them stood up shakily.

'We need to work fast,' whispered Portia.

With a real sense of urgency this time, they wove the thread in and out of the hammock, sewing it together just like the other one. The sailor inside was still sleeping like a baby when

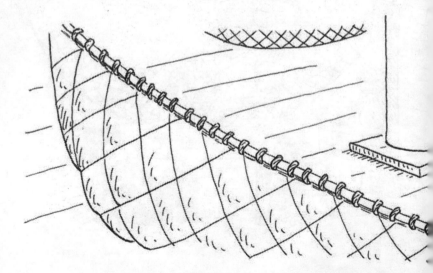

they'd finished, smiling to himself and sucking his thumb.

They stepped back to admire their handiwork.

'They look like cocoons,' said Jim, smiling.

'I wonder what sort of butterflies they'd turn into,' giggled Portia.

This time, Donnatella really did smile. She was actually feeling quite proud of herself.

'Well done, Donna!' said Portia, patting her heartily on the back. 'I told you you'd be fine. Anyway,' she went on, 'that's two more of Count Nasty's crew out of the way, but we need to sort out the last three before they come down here. Back to the storeroom and prepare for action!'

By the time the three of them arrived back at the storeroom, it was all prepared.

'We've got everything ready just as you asked us, Captain Portia,' said Emily, 'but what do we need the flour for?'

'You'll see in a minute,' said Portia. 'Just do like I said and cover yourselves in it, and make sure it goes in your hair. Who's got the boot polish?'

'It's over here,' said Peppermint.

'Right! When you've covered yourself in flour come over to me and I'll put the boot polish on.'

The ladies-in-waiting looked at each other as though Portia had finally gone mad.

'Trust me!' said Portia. 'It will all make sense in a minute!'

Jim picked up a handful of flour, dumped it on his head and started patting it into his hair and clothes. Everyone followed his example until the whole room was one big cloud of flour. Even Squawk and Twiggy were covered!

'Now! Make a line in front of me when you're ready for the boot polish.'

Soon there was a slightly puzzled-looking line waiting patiently in front of Portia, quiet except for the odd sneeze. One by one, Portia smeared a little of the boot polish around their eyes, and soon everyone realised what Portia had in mind.

'They think this ship is haunted already,' she explained. 'Now it's time to make them certain!' The crew looked at each other and almost frightened themselves.

'We can use these empty flour tins to help us make spooky noises. Let's get the big fishing net, then we're ready to go. Donna, you and Chloe stay here and look after things until we get back.' Donna breathed a huge sigh of relief.

'Jim, go out and have a listen to what's going on out there.'

'Aye, aye, Captain P,' said Jim, and went outside.

Up on the main deck, the remaining crew were getting worried. Bones, Cookie and Sticks (the youngest and scrawniest of Count Nasty's crew) had decided to stick together for safety.

'It's just the three of us up here now,' said Bones, 'so if we stay together nothing can get us.' They were a pathetic sight. Three grown men huddled together, wobbling their way up and down the deck.

'If we keep goin' round and round the ship,' added Sticks, 'nothing will be able to creep up on us either.'

'Yes, I think we should keep moving,' agreed Cookie.

Jim heard their voices die away as they went up the stairs to the poop deck, continuing their tour of the ship. He motioned to Portia and the others to come out of the storeroom.

Portia spoke to the group. 'You two go to the other end of the main deck. I want you to take either end of the net and wait on opposite sides. Make sure you stay out of sight when they come back down the steps. Squawk, when Claire and Emily are in position, you fly up to the poop deck and scare them back this way. It shouldn't be too difficult, they're scared enough as it is, I expect Twiggy will help you.'

'Aye, aye, Cap'n P!' squawked Squawk, though he wasn't too happy about having Twiggy as his assistant.

'The rest of us will be ready for them as soon as they come back this way.' Portia looked around at her crew. 'OK, action stations, everyone. This is it!'

Claire and Emily crept into place and Squawk flew up to the poop deck, while Twiggy darted her way along the handrails on the side of the ship. Portia, Jim and the rest of the crew lay in wait for their prey.

Squawk swooped low over the poop deck, knocking off Bones' hat.

'It's that stupid bird again,' said Bones, picking his hat off the deck.

The others were looking up in horror, mouths open wide.

'What's wrong with you lot?' said Bones, looking at their faces. 'I know that wasn't a ghost, it was that Princess Portia's pesky parrot.'

'It's g . . . g . . . gone w . . . white!' said Cookie pointing a shaky finger up at Squawk, who'd perched on top of the sail.

'MEEEEOOWWWWL!' howled Twiggy, jumping
out in front of the three sailors, her floury fur
standing on end.

'AAAAAARRGHHH! GHOSTS!!' they all
screamed and ran down the steps to the main
deck. They stopped in the middle and stood in a
huddle, blubbering.

Portia and the others stepped out from the
shadows.

'*Whoooo!*' howled Jim into one of the flour tins as they advanced slowly. His voice echoed out of the empty container and sounded so scary that it even sent a shiver down Portia's spine.

'*Whooooooooooo!*' echoed everyone else. They walked forward slowly in a cloud of flour, arms raised like zombies.

'*Whooooooooooooooooo!*' They howled again. Bones, Cookie and Sticks watched in terror.

'M . . . M . . . M . . . Mummy!' wailed Sticks. Cookie tried to run but he, like the others was frozen by fear.

'Whooooooooooooooooooooooo!' They were getting closer now and Squawk and Twiggy had joined them. Portia signalled to the ladies-in-waiting carrying the lids of the flour tins and they started bashing them together and wailing like banshees. That was it! The three terrified sailors remembered how to move their legs, turned, and fled in the direction they had come from, only to be caught in the fishing net that Claire and Emily had stretched across the deck. Before they knew what

was happening, they were trapped like three
giant guppies in the net and were being dragged
down below, crying like babies.

There had been so much noise this time,

however, that even Count Nasty had woken up.

'What is all that racket?' he snarled. 'I'm trying to get some beauty sleep down here!' He put on his dressing gown and came out of the Captain's cabin.

But, to his surprise, the ship seemed deserted

and for a very brief moment, he wondered if something strange was going on.

'Huh! I bet they've sneaked off to snooze

somewhere. I'll teach them to sleep on the job!'
He picked up a mop and marched off in search of
the crew.

'What's this?' Count Nasty said to himself.
The whole deck was covered in fish and flour.
'What on earth has been going on?' Count
Nasty looked down at the mess. 'What do we
have here . . .' There, in the flour, he'd spotted
some footprints . . . and they were rather smaller
than those of his crew.

'I suppose you think you're clever, Princess Portia?'
he said, with an evil grin. Quietly, Count Nasty
followed the footprints. They took him down to
the storeroom, where Portia and her crew were
busily securing their new catch.

'Ha ha!' exclaimed Count Nasty, bursting into
the room.

There was a collective gasp as the ladies turned,
just in time to see Count Nasty grab Portia and
take her prisoner!

'*Now* I've got you!' he crowed. 'Untie my men
immediately!'

'Stay where you are!' ordered Portia. She
looked at Jim, who was trying not to smile.

'I don't know what you're smiling at, young
man,' growled Count Nasty, 'your Captain is my
prisoner now!'

'I don't *think* so!' said Portia. She wriggled one
arm free and grabbed for the rope dangling
above their heads. Jim leaped forward and they
both pulled on the rope as hard as they could.

'Aaaargh!' yelled Count Nasty as he flew into

the air and found himself dangling by one ankle
from the ceiling.

It looked hilarious and everyone, including his
own crew, fell about laughing.

Count Nasty was FURIOUS! He dangled
there going redder by the second.

'Don't worry, Count!' gloated Portia. 'We
won't leave you hanging around for too long!'

Chapter Twelve

Count Nasty and his crew spent an uncomfortable night locked together in the storeroom.

'Just you wait till we get out of here,' he warned them. 'You'll be sorry you laughed at me!'

First thing in the morning, Portia, Jim, Peppermint and the crew of the *Flying Pig*, bundled Count Nasty and his men into a rowing boat and set them adrift.

'There's a fishing line, some rock cakes and a barrel of water in there, so you'll be fine until someone picks you up,' said Portia.

'I'll get you, Princess Portia, you'll see! I'll be there wherever you go!' snapped Count Nasty.

'You'll have to find me first!' she said and waved goodbye as the *Flying Pig* sailed away.

'That was a lucky escape!' said Peppermint to her cousin.

'Nonsense!' said Portia. 'It was skill and team-work!' She smiled.

'You know, Portia, I'm not the only Princess that needed rescuing,' said Peppermint, breathing in the fresh sea air. 'I was just lucky that you're my cousin. It's a shame we can't help the others.'

'Maybe we can . . .' said Portia grinning. 'I've got an idea. Squawk, I've got a job for you!' She got out a pencil and paper and began to write. 'Take this to the Princess Daily News!'

ARE YOU A PRINCESS IN PERIL?
CONTACT
PARROT POSTBOX 999
PORTIA
THE PIRATE PRINCESS

'That should do the trick!' said Portia, as she watched Squawk take to the sky. 'Who knows who'll need rescuing next?'

VOYAGES

West

Princess
Peppermint
of
Pomerania

King Brian and Queen Selena
cordially invite you to
the marriage of their daughter
Princess Pandora
to
Prince Norman of Moronia
at 4p.m. in the Royal Chapel

R.S.V.P.